ROSEMARY
THE PACIFIER FAIRY

BY
LINDSEY COKER LUCKEY

ILLUSTRATED BY
LORA LOOK

When Katie was a little baby,

Rosemary the Pacifier Fairy came by.

She gave a special gift to Katie

With a bright twinkle in her eye.

"This is your paci," Rosemary did say,
"And it will be your very best friend.
Your paci will be with you every day.
Until you're big, the friendship won't end."

The fairy said, "But do not be sad,"
And gave Katie a kiss on the head.
"This is a good thing, not at all bad.
It will help other babies go to bed."

Katie loved her paci a whole lot,

And always kept it close by.

When Katie grew up to be a tot,

She still couldn't tell Paci goodbye.

When it was time for Katie to sleep,
Paci was there to say goodnight.
When Katie woke up from her sleep so deep,
Her paci made everything all right.

When Katie's tummy started to roar,
She kept Paci 'till she could eat.

If Katie sat grumpily on the floor,
Paci helped her get back on her feet.

Katie used Paci every single day.

She loved Paci with all of her heart.

But like Rosemary the fairy did say,
Katie and Paci soon grew apart.

Katie had become a big girl,
And didn't need Paci all the time.
Now she could run, play, sing, and twirl,
And only used Paci at bedtime.

Soon Katie could sleep all by herself,

And play outside without a tear.

And as Paci sat on Katie's shelf,

What she must do became clear.

Katie could now send Paci on its way.

So, Rosemary came back that night.

"You are a brave girl," the fairy did say.

"Paci will help another sleep tight."

Katie gave one last kiss to her friend.

Then the fairy flew high in the sky.

Katie was sad their friendship must end,
But because she was big, she knew why.

Now that Katie and Paci were apart,

A new baby could keep Paci close by.

Even though Paci was in Katie's heart,

It was time for them to say goodbye.

Katie could make someone else smile,

And that was the right thing to do.

She got to love Paci for quite a while.

Paci would make another happy too.

Knowing she'd make someone feel good

Made Katie very happy too.

She had done all that she could

To give a baby joy till they grew.